Bits of Wit

and

Tons of Puns

HERBERT FIELD

PAGE PUBLISHING, INC.
New York, NY

First originally published by Page Publishing, Inc. 2017

ISBN 978-1-68409-865-1 (Paperback)
ISBN 978-1-68409-866-8 (Digital)

Printed in the United States of America

A Collection of Over

500 Puns & Other Nonsense

This book is dedicated with a warm heart to my children and grandchildren who are a constant inspiration in my life

About the Author

Herbert Clinton Field III was born and raised in Martinsville, Virginia. At an early age, and for unknown reasons, he was dubbed with the nickname "Piney," a mark of identity that has remained with him through the years. "Piney" attended Woodberry Forest School in Virginia and graduated from Duke University. At Duke, he became a world-class sprinter and was a four-year letterman in football. Following graduation, he received a commission in the US Air Force, serving on active duty for two years. He subsequently began a forty-year career in the furniture industry, holding marketing positions with several Virginia manufacturers. During that time, he was elected to the board of directors of the Southern Furniture Manufacturers Association. After retiring, he and his wife, Kitty, moved to her hometown of Edenton, North

Carolina, where he taught school for ten years. In Edenton, he began writing as a hobby, resulting in *Bits of Wit and Tons of Puns*. This is his first book. "Piney" and Kitty have four children and eight grandchildren.

One

Once a pun a time...

There was a nineteenth-century preacher who rode from village to village delivering Sunday talks on horseback. The people called this the sermon on the mount.

When Dracula was asked to explain some of his wretched deeds, he said he was not a count-able-to.

The young girl ate nothing but beef for a whole year and gained eighty pounds. What a Miss Steak!

Middle-aged man to middle-aged girlfriend, "What's that you have on tonight that smells so good?" "A hearing aid," she replied, "but I didn't know you could smell it."

The gnome was able to capture the gnu because it was taking a gnap.

Once the unmarried princess became queen, she called for an immediate mandate.

After Tonto encountered financial difficulties, the loan arranger became his best friend.

The sheriff had the neatest yard in town. He always insisted on lawn order.

She allowed her husband to stop by the bar one day a week. He usually went thirsty.

When the barbarians told the captive they were going to cut out his tongue, he said, "Well, I'll tell you one thing. I'm going to keep my mouth shut about this."

The snake charmer knew all of his subjects were poisonous. So why asp for trouble?

The diva with laryngitis was devastated when the media said her next presentation would probably be a hoarse opera.

After she married the meticulous dresser, she found out he was better at changing attire than he was at changing a tire.

The new 11:00 p.m. television rage all about watching calories: The Weight Weight Show.

A lady ordered a package of laxative at the drug counter. "Would that be for here or to go?" the spacey clerk asked.

The Little League pitcher was suddenly jerked out of the game in the seventh inning. His mom dragged him home and made him finish cleaning his room.

When asked if he would like to be an organ donor after he was dead, he said, "You can go ahead and haul that old pump organ out of the attic now. You don't have to wait until I'm dead."

The posse continued to fire at the outlaw as he slid off his horse into a pool of sewage. The poor fellow was shot in the waste.

Charlie was getting clobbered in a check-ers game by a man he despised. The fellow said,

"Okay, Charlie, you can crown me again." So Charlie picked up an umbrella and crowned him.

The bank employee was asked why their interest rates were so high. She said she wasn't a teller.

Dad was explaining billiards to his young son. "And this is a cue stick," Dad said. Son asked, "How in the world does Mom ever clean out her ears with that thing?"

The fourteen-year-old girl couldn't decide what flavor to make her first pie. It ended up being a lemon.

Boris to Horace: "What do you think the locals will say when they hear the government

is going to use their land to build a reservoir?"
Horace: "Dam."

The fellow did not believe in flying saucers until his wife discovered someone's lipstick on his shirt.

After several trips to the urologist, the fellow was finally given a blotter for his bladder.

The science class wanted to go stargazing, particularly to see Venus and Mars. Their teacher said, "Okay, we'll planet together."

When the town drunk got dressed up like a billy goat and crashed the club's masquerade ball, they threw him out by his goat tail.

Mom's quartet of boys all ended up in the Navy. She called them the four sea sons.

He was about to lose his cool over the constant demands of his lazy wife. "Get me a towel before I freeze," she yelled from the shower. "What color?" he asked.

He had an idea that the Pacific was deeper than the Atlantic, but it was just a notion.

To the compulsive gambler, paradise is a pair of dice.

After a questionable penalty, the coach screamed at the referee, "You stink!" The official promptly walked off fifteen more yards and yelled back, "How do I smell from here?"

Could you call a swordfish a sea saw?

The guy was very unhappy with his work selling shoes. He called it a hate-to-five job.

When she got tipsy at the club dance, he held her tight.

The trophy wife came to the party adorned in a silver necklace with matching bracelets and earrings. One guest remarked to his wife, "I thought you said she was a gold digger."

When the golf club sponsored a Scotch Foursome, very few of the players made it past the ninth hole.

The dairy bar was so crowded they were in need of some ice cream clones.

Some people in Florida were trying to form a protective agency for alligators. Do you think they were talking about Gatorade?

The card shark had one ironclad philosophy. It was, in fact, I deal.

After fifteen years of drinking his wife's vile coffee, he asked his lawyer if that was grounds for divorce.

The ex-burlesque dancer joined the military and ultimately was promoted to sergeant, but she had already earned her strips.

The Air Force pilot overshot his landing and ended up in the base garbage dump. It was a trash landing.

Before she got married, she told her friends she would not have over three children, and she ended up having six. She was kidding all the time.

The new couple were having a hard time accepting life in the nudist colony. One member said, "Just bare with us for a while."

The children started fibbing so badly their mom turned into a virtual lying tamer.

When the cops saw the known shoplifter with a wrap around his neck, they knew one thing. They knew it was stole.

The three teenagers didn't mind sharing a bathroom with their grandpa because it took him only a few seconds to brush his tooth.

They were invited to stay with a cousin for the reunion. She said there was plenty of room for them to sleep on the second floor. It was their first time sleeping on the floor.

The local ladies' man liked to love 'em and leave 'em. He believed in life, liberty, and the happiness of pursuit.

After a hectic morning session, the judge roared out to the rowdy courtroom, "Order in the court." Most of them ordered cheeseburgers.

He followed his wife for thirty minutes as she selected veggies at the fresh market. When she asked if he would like anything, he said, "I think I'll take a leek."

Patrolman to apprehended speeder, "Do you know how fast you were going?" Irate driver replied, "Any idiot knows you can't watch the road and speedometer at the same time." Speaking of idiots.

After considerable knee discomfort, she went to a specialist. He checked out her knee, shook his head, and asked, "What's a joint like this doing in a nice girl like you?"

A farmer was arrested for excessive speeding while transporting two donkeys to his farm. The sheriff told the judge, "He was really haulin' ass."

The golfer told his wife he had a hole in one, and she was overjoyed. Too bad he was talking about his socks.

After Leo and Virgo had a terrible fight, Virgo went to Pisces.

The Hatfields and McCoys once tried to work their farms together, but to no avail. There was just too much feud for them to handle.

After having a martini with James Bond, the young lady said she was stirred but not shaken.

When the preacher was told that termites had infested the entire foundation of the church, he said, "Let us spray."

As she was preparing for a TV debate, the aging candidate told the makeup artist, "Don't make me too pretty. I don't want to look like a beauty queen." "Don't worry," he replied.

The cowboys and Indians had a bloody fight during which most of the cowboys were massacred. They were, in fact, "headed off" at the pass.

When he met the glitzy American blonde in Europe, he asked, "How long have you been a broad?"

As recorded in a Swiss legend, William Tell shot an apple from his son's head using bow and arrow. According to one account, he did it without a quiver.

What Colonel Mustard said to the cast of *Clue* when he hit back-to-back jackpots at the casino: "Looks like I'm finally on a roll."

If you went skinny-dipping in Paris during the wintertime, some people might suspect you were in Seine.

The family's trip to Grandma's took four hours with no stops. But they did pass by a putrid-smelling sulfur plant that the parents jokingly referred to as the children's gas station.

After changing the twins' diapers for the fourth time that day, she said to her husband, "The more things change, the more they stay the same."

Four golfers were teeing off in the snow when they noticed some hunters in an adjacent field. One golfer said, "Look at those crazy fools, bird hunting in the snow."

Teacher is explaining usage of a metaphor: "Following the slow-moving cows through the narrow pasture, the short-legged mules were suddenly high-stepping stallions." Student says, "Looks like the cows knew what to use a meadow for."

Definition of *diverse*: a passage from the Bible often read at funerals.

The sexy redhead was well known for working the Reno casinos. She was a regular slut machine.

She was very miffed when she had to get out of a nice hot shower to answer the phone. All she had on was a scowl.

The doctor wanted to remove his spleen, but the fellow had reservations about an inside doubt job.

He took his weekly bath very faithfully every Saturday. His wife said it made her Saturday night live.

After being seated at the worst possible location in the cafe, the couple were left to whine and dine.

He refused to go on a diet. He said he'd just as soon die from what he et.

The high school sweethearts chewed gum constantly. When they smooched, it turned into a lot more lips stick.

As the fifty-year-old woman was watching the news on TV, the program was suddenly interrupted by a hot flash.

Returning from a two-year expedition in Siberia, the explorer was asked what his next move would be. He said, "Cancel my subscription to National Geographic."

Mom asks her son, "What happened to April on our calendar?" He says, "I put it in the trash." She replies, "Sweetheart, school won't be over until June regardless of what you do with April."

When his number-1 sprinter finished last in the hundred meter dash, the coach called it a half-fast effort.

After Paul Revere told his wife the British were coming, she asked, "Will they be here for dinner?"

The obnoxious stranger charged into the middle of the hunting party claiming the quail on the ground was his. So they gave him the bird.

When the star basketball player dunked donuts, he needed goggles and a bib.

In the frenzied excitement of a women's dress sale, one lady began to swoon and fainted. A friend said she got carried away.

The thirty-eight-year-old had the distinction of being the oldest bald player on the team.

They asked Sarah Palin to give her opinion on the best state of the union address in the past ten years. She said, "Alaska."

When the pirates told the captive to walk the plank, he asked, "Is there any possibility I could just walk the walk and talk the talk?"

The client asked for a spec sheet on his proposed home, but he wasn't expecting a description of bird droppings on the house.

When he fell and fractured his leg on the slippery floor at the laundry, it turned out to be a clean break.

The bride and groom left the church and headed directly to the airport. They had made plans to go to Hawaii and definitely wanted to fly united.

Jack asked Mack, "What do you think the chances are that skinny girl from the convent will ever get married?" Mack replied, "Slim and nun."

The near middle-aged woman was spending more and more time primping in front of her dressing table. It was a vanity thing.

The recipe for that wonderful cake they served originated in Outer Mongolia. It's called the Gobi dessert.

Following a champagne party on the cruise ship, the couple persuaded the very reluctant young captain to marry them. The sign on their suite read "Probably Just Married."

Mom accidentally added an acrid aloe to the butter in her pancake mix, but her loving son consoled her by saying he really liked the bitter butter batter better.

The five-foot six-inch coach was having a communication problem with his seven-foot center. "Hey, Mel," he said to his assistant, "go get me a stepladder."

A lady in Montreal told her neighbor that her daughter was moving "Way Down South"— to New York City.

The kid says, "Daddy, my teacher says global warming will raise temperatures half a degree a year." Dad replies, "Wonderful. Sixty years from now, we can get rid of our furnace."

A golfer was knee deep in brush looking for his ball. His buddy yelled, "Don't worry about snakes. There's no snake in its right mind that would go in there."

Teacher says to students on a field trip, "Is that a daisy or a nasturtium?" One student says, "Nasturtium." Teacher says, "Okay, write that down in your notebook." Student says, "It's a daisy."

Husband returns home from grocery store. Wife says, "Put those grapes in a bowl. I like to pick at them all day." "Why?" he responds. "You've already got me."

After four gallons of lemonade were consumed at the three-year-old's birthday celebration, it turned into a birthday potty.

When she caught her husband cheating, he begged her forgiveness and told her how much he loved her. It was a real SOB story.

Guilty defendant tells judge, "I was used, abused, accused, and confused." Judge responds, "So you're going to have eighteen months of confinement to bemoan, and atone all alone on your own."

He hated the monthly family get-togethers. It was a matter of too much kin dread.

A streetwalker was having a hard time making ends meet, so she joined a musical group. The strumpet played a trumpet.

The teacher asked a boy in class to use the words *detail*, *defeat*, and *defense* in a single sentence. He thought for a minute and said, "De feet go over de fence before de tail."

According to one old-time limerick, the lady from Niger rode on the back of a tiger. Makes you wonder how long she'd been out of the nuthouse.

When the young fellow was told in Sunday school to love his neighbor, he asked, "Which one? I got 'em living on both sides."

The punch-drunk boxer was preparing for his next match, desperate to get rid of the butterflies in his stomach. His trainer finally had to grab the insecticide out of his hand.

Most of the young sailors were seasick from trying to right the ship during a storm. So when the order came to heave to, they didn't need to be told.

Mick and Mack were discussing Mack's recent wedding. Mick said, "A very tender ceremony. I noticed a lot of people crying." "Yeah," Mack replied. "I was one of 'em."

Jim says to Walter, "I hear your granddad passed away. Was it unexpected?" Walter responds, "No, he was a hundred and sick."

When the men's clothing store closed at the mall, one fellow remarked, "Now it's a one-shop stopping center."

They told the cocktail party crowd to come early because of a storm threat. That was followed by some pretty heavy pre-sip-a-tation.

In an effort to expand his show and increase his daring acts, the trapeze artist began to go hire and hire.

When they put the harness around the pig, someone called it a boar constrictor.

The son screamed to his mom, "Mama, there's a huge snake in the den!" "Well, take it outside and kill it," she replied. "Don't you dare mess up my new carpet."

Two

They were desperately trying to get water into the mouth of their fellow hiker who had collapsed. He sat up and said, "Thanks a lot, but I really prefer unsweetened tea."

The family had to keep an eye on their collie and their favorite tree. They knew what the dogwood do.

The seventy-year-old woman insisted on dressing fifties style. Obviously, the fifties were her garb age.

Doctor says to patient, "So you're having severe headaches, chest pains, stomach cramps, shoulder spasms, and numbness in your arms. Remind me to check your legs next visit."

Husband calls wife and tells her he's going to stop and pick up ramen alfredo for dinner. Spacey wife asks, "And what would you like me to fix for Mr. Alfredo?"

After the socialite failed to get an invitation to the governor's ball, she felt absolutely list less.

Obnoxious football star asks the school beauty queen, "What's the chance of us getting together?" "Oh," she replies, "about one out of two." He smiles. She adds, "Million."

When he and the town gossip were given the job of serving ice cream at the neighborhood block party, he got the scoop.

Wife suspects husband is having an affair with his secretary. "So how long have you been sleeping with her?" she asks. He replies, "We really haven't been doing a lot of sleeping."

They had the country opry while they were still harvesting crops. It was corn on the job.

Jealous ex-husband asks current hubby, "So how do you like being married to a used wife?" He answers, "It's really not too bad once you get past the used part."

When the families began to bicker at the afternoon outing, the picnic became a nitpick.

She woke up at 2:00 a.m. after a wild dream about being pursued by a medieval suitor, so she decided to call it a knight.

Two intellectual introverts got married. Since they were both overweight, the affair turned into a big, fat geek wedding.

As the game between the Cleveland Indians and Atlanta Braves was about to begin, the umpire told the two managers, "Gentlemen, start your Injuns."

The new boss axed so many employees they started calling him the fire chief.

A restaurant in Texas had a large sign reading, "T-bones, 0.95." The fine print read, "With meat, 16.95."

Greta said to Golda, "You know, those sailors we met last night weren't too bad." Golda responded, "Ah men."

The shore bird flew around the fishing boat for a while before supping on the day's catch. He was just waiting for his tern.

When the robbery suspect proved he was not in the alley by the bank, the alibi saved him.

The trio of goody-two-shoes at school was known as the three little prigs.

As the youngster was finishing his recital of all the books in the New Testament, it was a revelation.

Why did the chicken cross the road? Actually, she didn't quite make it. All they ever found were a few feathers.

The house painter accidentally took in a mouthful of paint sealer. As they were taking him to ER, one medic told him to keep a stiff upper lip.

When the couple found a tarantula crawling around in their cookware, he said, "Let's skillet."

The handsome actor had many starring roles in his younger days, but once he started growing old, he became a movie idle.

The viola player and the violinist finally got together. She decided to string along with him.

After peroxide was accidentally spilled in the test lab, the technicians came up with three blond mice.

The not-too-bright teenager was disappointed with her first computer. She thought she would be able to dry her clothes on line.

When he stole the pig out of the pen, he didn't figure on being the one to end up in the pen.

Cy, our fat neighbor, went to college and joined a fraternity. Would you believe he pledged Psi Eta Pi?

The German was told that his forefathers liked their gin and tonic, but were careful about consumption. He thought of them as Teutonic drinkers.

When the house caught on fire while he was taking a shower, he made it out—barely.

A strong wind left the swinging bridge hanging as hikers were crossing a ravine, causing the excursion to be suspended.

Travel agent to customer: "Ma'am, on this travel visa, you need to put something other than *heaven* as your final destination."

The broker told the new agents they would be expected to sell not just a few houses, but lots and lots.

The daughter of the cruise ship's captain had always been a wonderful student. When she took a plunge off the honor roll, he became C sick.

When the PTA passed out free supplies at a Philadelphia school, it was truly pencil mania.

The valedictorian's name was pronounced incorrectly at the graduation because of the dean's lisp.

They retired the pro star's jersey and said the number would never be worn again. Someone asked, "How about the five hundred thousand that were sold in retail stores?"

A cop asked the escapee's mother if she knew where her son was, and she said, "Why, uh." He then asked, "Now is that Why uh oming or Why uh kiki?"

She didn't fit in very well with her peers. While they were scanning fun things on their smartphones, she was canning snap beans in the kitchen.

The Parisian streetwalker had a meeting with a gentleman to fulfill a business commitment. Just another French chore.

When the heir apparent was unexpectedly left out of his father's will, the devastated son said, "I just don't get it." "You're exactly right," a family member responded.

A diplomat is a person who can tell you to go to hell in such a way that you actually look forward to the trip.

The two knights were best friends, so when they dismounted each other in horseback combat, they both said it was joust in fun.

The herd's only two stags had a huge load during mating season. One ended up as a buck wasted and the other a buck well spent.

This girl had so many boyfriends she was called the pillow of the community.

The sales broker says he's tired of trying to sell houses and lots and is thinking about retiring to Florida. He's ready for some real escape.

The woman hounded her husband relentlessly to keep the leaves out of the yard. She always thought he was a rake anyway.

Joe ran into his ex-girlfriend with her new love at a party. He said, "I'd like to know what he's got that I ain't got." She replied, "Me."

When the caterer spilled all the wieners at the kennel club show, it turned into a dog-eat-dog affair.

The wannabe beach Adonis just didn't quite have it, but he did dig up enough clams to be called a mussel man.

When he met St. Peter at the Golden Gate and was given his keys to the kingdom, he asked if he could get a duplicate set for his wife.

The yeti lived in the brush and scrub for most of his young life. When he matured, he was overgrown.

She was fixing a breakfast surprise for the family, but it burned up on the stove. Turned out to be corned beef ash.

She told her son he had to take his homely cousin to the dance. Talk about cussin'.

The attendants were dressing the criminal for his hanging. They decided he would not need a necktie.

He mistakenly took his young son's suitcase on the cruise ship and found his Bermudas short.

The cocky rookie in the home run derby was bragging he would hit at least a dozen homers, but he only managed to get eight. He just didn't have balls enough to do it.

When a person is christened, is that water over the damned?

The eighty-eight-year-old said he felt as though he could drive a golf ball a mile, so he put a ball in his pocket and rode his cart around the course.

Two fellows were discussing the town character, and one said, "That old man's half crazy." The other added, "Well, it's too late to turn back now. He might as well go for it."

After someone told the Dolphins' cheerleader she was the most beautiful girl in town, she responded, "My, am I?"

After he lost half of their savings at the racetrack, the TV weatherman was told by his wife, "My forecast for tonight: very cool."

The kids went to a coed camp, and the fellows swooped in and got the last cabin with beds. You might say the girls were boycotted.

Father asks his daughter, "Sweetheart, what time is your doubles match tomorrow?" Daughter answers, "Tenish."

She asked, "Now that your grandpa has dentures, how are his eating habits?" He replied, "Oh, he can manage to get down most anything he chews-es."

The US Marine fell asleep in the sun right in the middle of Florida's citrus country. When he woke up, he was a tan gyrene.

When the baby doctor helped to develop a more efficient type of diaper, he gained considerable stature as a pee-diatrition.

Desperate message sent out by the people in the Alamo when their sewage system failed: "Mission impossible."

Following a pilot's report that a stewardess was on a controlled substance, one of the investigators asked, "Well, how high was she?" The pilot replied, "Thirty-two thousand feet."

The family was sitting down to a birthday dinner for their adorable daughter. Their not-so-adorable son screamed out, "I don't have a fork!" Mom snapped back, "Well, it's not your birthday."

When the beauty queen insisted on wearing her very showy headdress to the afternoon social gathering, it was a tea-error.

Would you say Pinocchio's small dog would also be a pup pet?

The zoo curator brought in a cobra with a badly abscessed fang for treatment. The vet decided a shot of penicillin would be quite adequate.

He walked his dog six blocks to the vet for a urinalysis. The only trouble was they passed six fireplugs along the way.

The lonely lady lived far out in the country and had very little access to the news. So she attended a creative arts class and made herself a paper boy.

When the man got to heaven, he was told he would have to wait a little while before he could actually go in. He was left waiting in the wings.

The new mother was constantly complaining about the baby's spit up. Her husband finally commented, "Spit happens."

Obnoxious Jets fan spouts off at game in Boston, "I've been saving up for four days to go to the bathroom here." Prim Patriots follower replies, "You obviously haven't gone yet."

What you can count on for the winter solstice—autumn leaves.

Someone asked him if he closed his eyes when he kissed his sweetheart. "No," he said. "I always like to know what's going on under my nose."

The young couple decided to elope, and they left town pulling a mobile home behind them. The girl's father called it trailer hitching.

The fans from Pleasantville went to the big game at Podunk singing their team's praises. The home team followers chanted, "Go to hell." Someone from Pleasantville shouted back, "We're already there."

The broad strolled into the bar sporting a pair of forty-fours. She also wore two revolvers.

When the couple became stalled in traffic, they saw a "Slow Funeral" sign ahead. The husband grumbled, "Well, have you ever been to a fast one?"

That segment of the six o'clock news that deals with natural elements is really a whether report.

When Moses came down from Mount Sinai, he had just been informed what the ten commands meant.

This fellow wasn't sold on any certain political party, but did lean slightly to one side. He called himself a demi-crat.

After pranksters put *Tyrannosaurus rex* on the restaurant menu, it really was a diner's awe.

As the train raced around a curve late in the day, dinner was just being swerved.

The lady film director received a birthday surprise on the set. She cried out, "It's a wrap."

While his wife went shopping on Christmas Eve, he found a holiday's ale.

The boys in the fraternity surprised the sorority with a panty raid. The girls retaliated in a mad tirade.

After the royal family landed at the Madrid airport, the king and his son did not appear immediately. The band played "The Reign in Spain Stays Mainly in the Plane."

Question to PE class: Who did the most to popularize polo around the world? Freshman answer: Marco.

When invited to attend a function at the home of a woman she detested, she replied that she had already made plans to be sick that day.

What they use to knock the ice off the runners of a luge: a sleds hammer.

Someone told a visitor that the coastal town was started as a haven for pirates, outlaws, and prostitutes, but one old-timer said he'd never heard anything about pirates and outlaws being there.

After the emergency surgery, the patient was very downcast, so the doctor told her a couple of jokes and left her in stitches.

The son really enjoyed coming back home to his mother's cooking. His very favorite was her bacon-and-cheese mom-elet.

He was sorry for losing his job. He was sorry for losing his wife. He was sorry for losing his friends. To tell the truth, the man was just plain sorry.

When the 280 pound man told the 200 pound woman he loved her, things really started getting heavy.

The teacher simply could not connect with the fourth grader. It was a class-sick case of boredom.

After the hurricane changed course just minutes away from a populated area, it was a wind-wind situation.

The farmer tried to dig through the hard ground for water, but it turned into an irritation project.

After following her mother around the golf course, the six-year-old described *putting* as hitting the ball as many times as possible without letting it fall in the hole.

During the latter days of the chase, Captain Ahab was hoping the whale would turn into a mopey Dick.

When the enemy nations met for peace negotiations in the desert, the sessions were intense.

The boxers beat themselves brutally for fifteen rounds and then went out to dinner together. Do you think they had black-eyed peace?

The girl worked for years on the family's melon farm with little hope of ever finding a husband. All she ever heard around the house was "Can't elope, can't elope, can't elope."

Son asks dad at baseball game, "What's wrong with our ace pitcher?" Dad responds, "What do you mean?" Son says, "They just announced he was throwing up in the bullpen."

The students asked what it would have cost per person to cross the Atlantic with the pilgrims. Teacher said, "About $4 a galleon."

He really didn't want to go to Brazil and work for the coffee company, but there were so many perks he just couldn't turn the job down.

When the Catholic clergyman from New York was told he was being transferred, he said he would like to be a St. Louis Cardinal.

The Norwegian fisherman was in dire need of a new truck. He finally found a good deal on a fjord pickup.

After locusts swarmed all over the farm, the place looked like the Garden of Eaten.

Nick asked Mike, "Did Lois Schidtsel ever manage to get her name changed?" Mike answered, "Yeah, she changed it to Betty."

One thing you can say about the candidate who ran against George Bush in 2004: He was a real goer.

Father says to son, "That's the second time you've been bitten by that dog. The first time, it's his fault. The second time, it's yours." Son says, "Does the dog know that?"

This hardworking man spent the greater part of his life cleaning bathrooms in the schools. He was affectionately called the headmaster.

The artist made a great living using acid to produce beautiful glass pieces. He sold a lot of them for one thousand dollars ctch.

He preached to his son relentlessly about being a spendthrift, but when his daughter quit school and went to live a wasteful two years abroad, he realized he had a prodi-gal.

Their love affair was getting to the boiling point. Every time they got ready to kiss, their lips were already forming at the mouth.

When he married Liza, they weren't sure about children, but after three in four years, he said, "She's like fertile Liza."

Two neighbors were having a heated argument about their property line. One asked, "Well, what are you going to do about it?" The other answered, "Try to figure out how to deal with a mule-headed jackass."

Son says, "Dad, this pile of dog do needs to go to the garbage bag." Dad replies, "Well, what are you waiting for? Give it to your mother."

When the rider was thrown from his mount crossing a small stream, the horse ran away. The fellow found himself up the creek without a saddle.

Three

The teenage girls loved to flirt with the older surfers at the beach, but all they ever got was a big wave.

"Waitress," he said, "I ordered a BLT. What is this I got?" "You got a BLT," she replied. "Bagel, lox, and tea."

Following the execution, nobody paid much attention to the outlaw. He was just kinda hanging around.

The curse of Frankenstein: When the monster's ear came loose and disappeared into a drainage ditch.

When mom came breezing in with lemonade at her daughter's first teen party, she was really checking necking and pecking.

The Buffalo resident thought she saw a Nessie in the water. She must have been looking at Lake Eerie.

Two teachers put on a mule's costume for the school play. They really made a jackass out of themselves.

This three-hundred-pound man ordered a double cheeseburger and fries for lunch. And a diet cola

The schoolkids in the neighborhood call the garbage truck their weekly reeker.

Eighty-year-old to eighty-year-old: "They're going to remove my gallbladder next week." Response: "Heck! Wish I'd thought of that. What a way to lose weight."

When the librarian was charged with absconding with funds from the media center, the judge threw the book at her.

The eleven-year-old asked the twelve-year-old, "Have you ever seen Mars?" "Nope," he replied, "but I've seen Pa's.

When the alteration service lost the groom's formal wear on the morning of the wedding, the bride turned ashen and swooned. The tailor was even paler.

The tribe couldn't think of a name for their new chief, but after he wandered in front of the target during archery practice, he became known as Chief Arrowhead.

Wife to husband at wedding: "Your daughter would like to stand near the aisle and blow kisses at the bride and groom when they leave." Husband: "Well, you'd better tell her to blow her nose first."

As she was preparing to leap off the sinking ship, the woman asked a sailor, "Do you recommend the breaststroke or the Australian crawl?"

What his wife might do if he continues to miss his bank payments: eat a loan.

What's the difference between a zebra and a Z bra? You can see a zebra in a zoo. Chances are, no one will ever see a Z bra.

Batman didn't really care what position his son played on the baseball team just as long as he wasn't called the batboy.

The cowboy who was lost on the prairie was hungry enough to eat a horse. Unfortunately, his horse was hungry enough to eat a cowboy.

The ET took one look at Las Vegas and said, "And I thought we were far out."

When the shy suitor sent a FedEx to propose to his girlfriend, it was the best way he knew to express his feelings.

Should old acquaintance be forgot and never brought to mind? Sometimes that ain't a bad idea.

After a quick bowl of hasty pudding, the hair growing on his upper lip looked like a mush stash.

There was a student who had to spend his summer with a tutor because of poor geometry grades. He felt like he'd been put in a prism.

The fifteen-year-old had just gotten her learner's license and was doing her best to control the car, but as a driver, she was still a little wet behind the gears.

There was an argument about who had won the poker pot. Someone pulled a gun, and this fellow was shot in the heart, dead certain he had the winning hand.

The child's parents complained that their son had been cut short on the octopus ride. "Relax, folks," the attendant said. "He can go again. It's not the end of the whirl."

Husband to wife: "What has four arms, four legs, eats everything in sight, and lives in a pile of dirt?" Wife's reply: "Oh, you mean the twins."

The family hated to take their tobacco-chewing grandpa on a long trip because he had to make too many spit stops.

As the oldest member in a long lineage of wealthy relatives, the fellow was jokingly referred to as an heir head.

The ballerina was an expert doing the pirouette, but after going through three husbands, she was obviously also pretty good at trap dancing.

The young employee failed to move up the corporate ladder because he schlepped too much on the job.

When the sketch artist ran out of the hotel without paying his bill, the drawer left his drawers in a drawer.

The scoundrel beat his wife and embezzled money but was eventually put in prison, which proves that time wounds all heels.

The young pastor was about to be married, but instead left town and went on a religious crusade. The wannabe bride called it preach of promise.

She could not stomach rare meat. So when she finished her steak at her boyfriend's first cookout, she hugged him and said, "Well done."

The spokesman for a well-known chicken fast-food chain is viewed by some as a colonel of com.

There was a huge turnout for the family reunion and picnic where the ants definitely outnumbered the uncles.

The first grader started slipping into the bathroom and using his dad's razor. He was just a little shaver.

The teenage girl was being pursued by a romantic classmate. She couldn't stand him. Every time he came to the door, it was a real pain in the knock.

The new neighbor asked, "Do you have a problem with moles here?" The old-timer answered, "We did, but the snakes ate them, and the alligators took care of the snakes."

Wife asks her husband, "Have you been drinking?" He replies, "Well, I had coffee for breakfast, tea for lunch, two bottles of water, and, oh yeah, a six-pack on the way home."

The couple were swimming in a secluded lagoon. She said, "I like it when you put your arm around me like that." He answered, "But I don't have my arm around you."

The miner knew he couldn't smoke on the job, but he was counting on a light at the end of the tunnel.

A newcomer to a hunting club asked about a member who was a notoriously poor shot. "How do we know what he's shooting at?" he inquired. Someone said, "Just duck."

The fugitives who were being hunted by the police were in the middle of the copse the whole time.

Flying his wife and two children to Europe, he realized air-fair was anything but.

After a disastrous meal in their igloo, the Eskimo family decided not to have tuna melt again.

Hangings were so prevalent in the Old West that weekly publications were full of nothing but obituaries. Some people called them noose papers.

The aspiring lawyer had a terrible time passing the bar because he seldom did.

Two women decided to go rabbit hunting with their husbands, but they came home empty-handed. Turned out to be a bad hare day.

A famous movie star owns a very successful car-leasing business. He calls it Burt Rentals.

The senior class is always complaining about having their food thrown at them by the sloppy servers in the cafeteria. The kindergarten class doesn't complain. They throw it back.

When he asked his beautiful classmate if she wanted to go out with him, she said, "I do." Unfortunately for him, what she was really saying was "Adieu."

The flaky Romeo was getting married for the fourth go around. He figured it was time to change his wife style again.

After the teen's mom received numerous compliments for the wonderful breakfast she provided for the sleepover, she was on a huge Eggo trip.

The traveler from New York stopped in a southern restaurant and ordered a huge country-style breakfast. After stuffing himself thoroughly, he had his regrits.

This man was beginning to worry about his wife's safety. She belonged to so many civic and social organizations he was afraid she was going to be clubbed to death.

The doctor had received no immunization and was being exposed to viruses every day, so he shot himself in the foot.

His wife was always complaining about their sloppy garbage pickup. He kept telling her, "You can't fight city haul."

The seventy-eight-year-old woman and the eighty-year-old man met in the hospital. After they got out, they considered marriage but weren't sure about their joint holdings.

When the lead vehicle in the burial procession broke down, they had to go back and re-hearse the funeral.

Her phone rang, and a man's voice said, "Hello, darling, I just wanted to tell you what a wonderful time I had with you last night." She responded, "Who is this?"

The cannibals raved about the English lord they captured in the jungle. They said he was a man of extremely good taste.

The driver of a gas truck told his buddy he was planning to enter his rig in an upcoming road race, but he was just fueling around.

While the young Native American was helping to move the family emblem, he realized why it was called a totem pole.

What to expect at dawn: raise of sun.

The student was reading his book report aloud to the class and was getting a hilarious response. His teacher quickly came over and whispered, "Zip your pants up."

Grandpa didn't have a full set of dentures, so he had to do the best he could when it was upper time.

Son tells his mom he's heading out to an evening jazz concert. "Will you be late?" she asks.

"No, ma'am," he answers. "It ought to be over by two or three."

The divorced hubby returned home unannounced to pick up a few items of clothing, but after an encounter with his ex, all he got was a couple of socks.

He took his wife Christmas shopping but wasn't sure what she wanted. However, he soon found out what she went fur.

The theology student was an excellent basketball player. He was also excellent at juggling his playing time with his praying time.

Wife unloads on impossible husband, "You're the laziest, lousiest crumb in existence. I'm going to Palm Beach and move in with mother." "Can I go too?" he asks.

Ben asks Frank, "How was your twenty-two-hour flight to China?" Frank replies, "A boring 777."

Inmates at the state prison call the recreation area their playpen.

The postman says his job is very stressful because he's always pushing the envelope.

Their science teacher was giving an in-depth explanation about nuclear fission. One student whispers to another, "If she's so darned smart, why does she want to be a schoolteacher?"

He asked his wife where she was going, and she said, "To a fair." He followed her.

When the father of five girls went to the maternity ward, he exclaimed, finally, "Oh boy."

It was a dark and stormy night in the mountains, but the locals were happy. They had plenty of moonshine.

The Spanish galleon was transporting a load of farm animals to the starving colonists. When attacked by pirates, the captain roared out, "Don't give up the sheep!"

When he told the cook he was not particularly fond of her sweet yam concoction, he was being quite candid.

The British knight was given an unexpected award by the queen. It was a true sir prize.

The new candy craze in Hollywood is the la la pop.

She called the new pastor to come to dinner and asked if chicken fricassee would be suitable.

The reverend chuckled and said, "I've never met a chicken I didn't like."

The World War II veterans were reminiscing at a reunion. "I'll never forget the crazy names of some of those German towns," the fellow from Poughkeepsie said to the guy from Punxsutawney.

The arsonist had a real flare for causing alarm.

The referee approached the coach. "You're starting twelve men. That's a penalty." The coach grimaced and replied, "If you knew how bad they were, you'd penalize the other team."

"Son," the father said, "if someone hits you, turn the other cheek." The young fellow thought for a minute and asked, "Uppcr or lower?"

When the two scientists were called on to approve the hospital's testing facilities, they co-lab-rated.

Recoil: What the snake decided to do when it realized it was lying on a four-lane highway.

The girl asked her boyfriend, "Have you had your teeth whitened?" "No," he said. "I just had a dose of milk of magnesia."

Fred: "I hear McPherson got pulled for speeding. Isn't he about ninety?" Mort: "Yeah, he heard Tom Watson shot his age in a golf tournament, and Mac was trying to drive his age."

She said, "You've got that root canal tomorrow. When do you want me to wake you up?" He answered, "Day after tomorrow."

What was the name of that one-of-a-kind creature often seen around Mayberry? An ant bee.

A bystander was hit in the head with a black-jack while witnessing a fight. The police arrived and took him to jail. It was a classic case of missed-de-meaner.

The patient complained that the cold pack on his shoulder was too much, but the flirtatious nurse cooed back, "Can't take my ice off of you."

Mom refused to change her hairdo after thirty years. The family called it mama's little curl.

When told they were having possum for dinner, the guests had thinks before they ate.

When he heard the road to hell was paved with good intentions, he wondered if he could just skip the good intentions and call it even.

His postage costs were going up. His deliveries were late. His mailings were not being received. He was really getting PO ed.

Think of all the churches that would have a different name today if Saul had not become Paul.

When the mole was discovered in the CIA, he said it wasn't his fault because they always kept him underground.

Addendum to well-known nursery rhyme: "Peas porridge hot, peas porridge cold. Peas porridge in the pot nine days old. Pee-yew!"

Young son asks dad for a pony. Dad says, "We don't have the money." Son counters with "But the ATM is full of money, and you get all you want every time we go."

The young boy asked his dad, "Why do they say love so many times in tennis? They play like they hate each other."

"George," she said, "will you please speak to your son about his atrocious eating habits and pass him a couple of napkins." George snorted, "How about a bath mat?"

The first grader came home perplexed. "Mom," he said, "my crazy teacher said a bull is a cowboy." Mom smiled and replied, "I'm sure she means a bull is a boy cow."

He spent thirty minutes at breakfast listening to his wife's instructions for the day. When he got up to leave, he said, "Good-bye, dear. If you call me, need me."

The middle-aged woman was beginning to be more and more conscious about the appearance of her backside, so she had a rearview mirror installed in her bedroom.

When the middle-aged man sat down in the barber chair and said he would like his hair to look like Clark Gable's in *Gone with the Wind*, the barber cried out, "Next!"

Four couples went for a long weekend; the men would be deer hunting, the women watching TV. So both groups had three days to kill.

The girl's father was an airline pilot and stayed in the air most of the time, so she called her mother's dad her ground dad.

The bootleggers found they couldn't hide much corn liquor in their outhouse. It was only a demijohn.

After a disastrous earthquake in Great Britain, the ground wasn't there any moor.

The weather report called for clear skies for the outdoor movie tryouts. But when they picked one hundred people for fifty roles, it turned into an overcast day.

The woman directed the cab driver to a convenience store and told him to wait for her. After fifteen minutes, he went inside and bellowed out to the cashier, "Have you seen my fare lady?"

She was serious. He was not. However, after she begged and begged him to give her a ring, he did call her the next day.

The girls' soccer team had consecutive tie games with identical scores after the second game ended up two to two too.

He never really understood the game of bridge but played because of his wife. Even when he wasn't the dummy, she sure made him feel like he was.

The dentist's son always tried to leave his customers with a satisfied smile when they left his filling station. Just like his dad.

As the opera star was receiving his ten-year sentence for tax evasion, his attorney put in a special request for Sing Sing.

The aspiring pilot was worried about having to solo on a very windy day. He finished in a breeze.

After the lazy student had to beg his way through four years of high school, he was presented with a gift certificate at graduation.

The family had nicknames for their motorbikes. They called their father's Pops-cycle.

After they cut half of the civic jobs in town, the governing group was referred to as the city cancel.

The twins were given their choice of jobs in the fruit-packing plant, so the pair pared pears.

The staff in ER experienced a new challenge when the three-year-old was brought in. They had to remove his finger from his nose.

When the dentist took one look into the mouth of the woman who had pyorrhea, he said,

"Your teeth are fine, but your gums will have to come out."

The man and woman left church because of an offensive odor. It was obvious they had gotten in the wrong pew.

This near genius in California developed a revolutionary process for stopping seepage in septic tanks. He's called the Wizard of Ooze.

A professor asked a student where he thought the least seismic activity was in the United States. The fellow said, "Little Rock."

The young marrieds were absolutely carried away with the arrival of their new baby daughter. "It's small," she said, smiling, "but we like it."

His wife was a terrible cook. When she scolded, "Will you stop eating like a pig," he responded, "If it's slop, you eat it like a pig."

There was a story about a dog swimming two miles downstream to retrieve a stick his master had thrown in the river. "Sounds kinda far-fetched to me," one fellow said.

After the man and his wife fought practically all night, they both woke up hungry. They kissed and made up, then sat down to harmony and grits.

When the three astronauts were crammed into a very tight compartment, one said to the others, "Welcome to out of space."

The coach usually got hungry sitting on the bench, so he always kept a couple of subs beside him.

The depleted utility department had only one worker who could control the town's water supply. He became the main man.

Pastor asks the groom, "Do you promise to love, honor, and obey her for the rest of your life?" Groom hesitates then asks, "What are my other options?"

Joe asked his friend, "Did your uncle require any help on his way to the top of the corporate ladder?" "No," the friend answered, "he learned how to lie and cheat all by himself."

When the plate umpire's finger was jammed by a tipped ball, what he yelled out was foul.

Four

"Is that thunder I hear?" Brad asked his teacher friend. "No," the teacher said. "It's the first day of practice for the middle school band."

The boy and his sister fought relentlessly. Finally, the parents told the boy he needed to practice a little more re-sis-tance.

He and his buddy had similar-sounding but different philosophies on marriage. His was "Why not?" His buddy's was "Why knot?"

Her face turned red when she had to go to the bathroom while they were dancing, but the flush was gone before she returned.

The doctor took out the midget's appendix with just a few snips of the scissors. It was a short cut.

When the retired minister was unexpectedly asked to fill in during the church outreach mission, he spoke for two hours. He thought they said outpreach.

Her new friend said he would like some gloves for his birthday, but she was looking for a beau tie.

There were so many new babies in the neighborhood someone suggested the diaper service ought to start using a dump truck.

When his new girlfriend told him "Lips that touch wine will never touch mine," he went out and bought a bottle of bourbon.

In addition to his *Origin of the Species* work, Darwin also sponsored a permanent body preservation ointment called Everlotion.

Very few of the baseball fans thought the game should have been called off because of a few sprinkles. They will remember it as rain doubt.

There is an addendum to St. Nick's contract with his elves that says they must retire at eighty-five. It's called Santa's clause.

When the country bumpkin stumbled into town with his first camera, he took pictures of everything in sight. You might say it was a photograph-hick experience.

She returned from the dance recital all excited. "You should see all of those early bloomers in that lineup," she said to her husband. "Are they still wearing those darned things?" he asked.

He asked her to be his date for the senior dance and then backed out. It was a prom missed.

When the Neanderthal boy reached sixteen, he was given his first weaponry for hunting and protection. His father said, "Welcome to the club."

When accused of stealing a bottle of liquor from the package store, the man refused to answer on grounds of self-incrimination. In other words, he took the fifth.

The aspiring young actor got a job in a Hollywood art warehouse. It was his start in moving pictures.

When he left her standing at the altar for the third time, she sang out, "You're the best thing that never happened to me."

Lightning struck a bandstand at an outdoor concert, and nobody was hurt. Everyone agreed they had a good conductor.

They refueled and had lunch at a truck stop. When they went to pay, they were told the gas goes with the meal.

The shortstop was taken out of the game because he didn't field well.

Their mother's sister made a fantastic ice dessert that the kids loved. They called it Aunty Freeze.

After retiring, the train engineer decided to become a psychiatrist. He'd always had a keen interest in loco-motives.

Bugs Bunny greeted Porky Pig with "What's up, Doc?" Porky answered, "Duh, duh, I don't know, Bugs. I never heard of updock."

When the divorcee went on a diet, she really missed her ex for breakfast.

During the heat of battle, the Scottish soldier became entangled in his own outer garment, and that's how he got kilt.

Friends are sure the new lumberjack is happy with his job because he ax like it.

After he stole the trumpet from the music store, he was apprehended almost immediately. The poor guy really blew it.

When the police surprised the gang of safe-crackers at the bank vault, it looked like scrambled yeggs.

Two one-hundred-year-olds try to get reacquainted at a reunion, but they can't shake hands because of their hands' shake.

What's the difference between a bus and a baby? A bus goes from city to city. Now where would a baby go to make that rhyme?

A businessman traveling in Chicago phoned a young lady he had met previously. He asked, "I was wondering if you'd be free tonight." "Sorry," she said. "It'll never be free."

I came up with a brand-new word. I simply call it *morange*. Please don't ask me what it means. It's just to rhyme with *orange*.

One six-year-old says to another, "My dad says he's tired of giving half of his paycheck to the Eternal Revenue Service."

Pre-Christmas refrain cheerfully flowing from seventh grade classroom: "Hark the herald angels shout, three more days, and we'll be out."

Those ancestors of ours who had to determine whether or not mushrooms were poisonous went through a lot of trial and terror.

A group of bootleggers were sampling a fresh batch of hooch and quietly enjoying themselves in the still of the night.

Dad says to young son, "I hear your team got beat 59–6." "Yeah," the son answers, "we had 'em. We just got careless in the fourth quarter."

After dating the girl for three weeks, he found that the only thing they had in common was a cold.

The teacher was reprimanded for wearing short shorts to class, but she argued that her job called for her to be in-form-ative.

Noah enjoyed giving his family nicknames while they were adrift on the floodwaters. He called one of his granddaughters Joan of Ark.

The best man at the wedding continued to toast the bride, the groom, the parents, the grandparents, until his wife finally told him to wine down.

When three of the football players were caught breaking training, there was a kickoff the day before the game.

The famous Edgar Allan enjoyed a truly brilliant writing career, but his life had a very Poe ending.

There was a sixth grader who drove his teacher crazy with rude and inconsiderate manners. He was a real pain in the class.

When neighbors asked the lady why she didn't stop her dog from chasing their cat, she said she couldn't leave the house because she had on only a negligee. Pretty flimsy excuse.

The noise from the baby ward in the hospital was bothering patients. A couple of the doctors said it was time to reevaluate their cry-teria.

Marge asks, "What do we call our new minister? He has a doctoral degree and all of that stuff." Mabel answers, "Just call him preacher. He already knows the rest."

The family had a black-sheep uncle who was a chain-smoker, habitual drinker, and lived the life of a slob. His existence was really in-crud-able.

When Grandpa hung lanterns and jingling bells on his horse's buggy, it turned into a folk's wagon.

The couple's small boat capsized and left them stranded on a lonely coral island for three days. They didn't seem to mind atoll.

Old neighbors meet after ten years. One mom says, "And I believe your Janie was two years older than my Susie." The other replies, "Yes, she still is."

If a steer mated with a mare, do you suppose their offspring might be a little hor-bull?

She dreaded going to the local butcher's. He charged too much and liked a nip or two in the morning. Suspicions were confirmed when she got there. He was way too high.

The stringent mom broke up the teen party early when she suspected the boys and girls were starting to get too-gether.

He was stunned when he opened the closet door and found that his formal jacket was riddled with moth holes. He knew a real tux-eater had been there.

Teenager asks his buddy, "What's your dad going to do when he finds out you got kicked out of class?" His buddy answers, "Beats the heck out of me."

Disgruntled husband complains to agitated wife, "There's no blasted toilet paper in here."

She replies, "There are twelve rolls in the closet. If you need more than that, I'll call the doctor for you."

Following surgery, the man was told he would need to change his eating habits or face more health problems. It was his post-opt.

This man was asked how his wife responded to her recent lip enhancement procedure. He said, "Let's just say when she eats an apple, she has to kiss it before she bites it."

When Cleopatra was accused of assassinating her brother, she refused to take the blame. She was, after all, Queen of de Nile.

What Jon gave Garfield for Christmas: a kitty car.

The youngster said he was well informed on the facts of life, but he was still trying to figure out what the birds and bees do.

She picked up her husband from work on payday and drove straight to the mall. He said it was the quickest way he knew to trash a check.

The pet beagle liked to chime in and try to carry a tune when the family sang together. They called him the hound of music.

Voting in most communist countries is usually over before it starts. In fact, they seldom have an election that lasts over four hours.

After ten years of agonizing, his wife finally broke him from dangling a toothpick out of the side of his mouth. She convinced him he looked better without the lip stick.

The doctors did an excellent job of joining a new valve to the patient's aorta. They expected him to fully recover from the heart attach.

There was a beautiful foreign spy suspect who was constantly being investigated by the FBI, but they were unable to convict her. She never had on any underwire.

The cows were discussing their personal problems. It was mostly about dis and dat and de udder.

When the reprobate came running out of the blazing house clad only in a shirt, he was true to form in burning his britches behind him.

Mom thought her teenage sons were finally growing up, but after some friends stopped by for a wild sleepover, she realized they were still litter boys.

The girl never fulfilled her ambition to have a military career, but she did manage to become a beautician in the hair force.

When David slew Goliath, he served notice that he was not a giant's fan.

The team's best runner was dreadfully overworked and generally worn out after the first thirty minutes of a game. He was, in fact, one good half back.

Two dermatologists dated for several years but finally broke up. They realized their affection was only skin deep.

After numerous tours of duty and many girlfriends, the army colonel finally retired, still single. He had been looking for love in all the wrong bases.

While taking a stroll, she spotted her neighbor's womanizing husband walking his dog and fast approaching from the rear. She turned around and called out, "Heel!"

Dad and son were discussing son's upcoming marriage and the fiancée's financial status. The son said, "Well, I can tell you one thing. She has a diamond mind."

The plates were being passed and filled for a sumptuous family dinner offering several kinds of meat. Mary had a little lamb.

The young couple were having a hard time raising a family on their limited budget. Too much month at the end of the money.

On Christmas morning in Richmond, Norfolk, and all over the state, there were no gifts from St. Nick. Someone sent a text to the North Pole, "Yes, Santa Claus, there is a Virginia."

This fellow went to the library to study, but other students continued to make distracting noises to get his attention. He was really getting psst.

The actress was walking around reading the manuscript for a short presentation. She accidentally bumped into an admirer, and the skit hit the fan.

They named their children Eenie, Meenie, Miney, and Joe. You're probably wondering, "Why Joe?" Because they didn't want any Mo.

The poor bartender had heard about so many husband-and-wife disasters he came up with a special drink he called Marriage on the Rocks.

Rhonda and Wanda were discussing Rhonda's husband. Wanda said, "I like Al, but isn't he a little bullheaded?" Rhonda replied, "Actually, you're talking about the wrong end of the bull."

Preacher calls on a widow late one night and says he wants to discuss the hereafter. She says, "If you're here after what I think you're here after, you're gonna be here after I'm gone."

When Santa left the bar on Christmas Eve, they gave him one for the road. They said they wanted him to have a drink on the house.

The umpire made an obviously stupid call, and all the players on the field converged on him. It turned into an ass-and-nine spectacle.

Mom queries daughter, "You say Grandpa was standing on the porch reliving himself. What in the world is that?" Daughter comes back with "I said he was relieving himself."

They asked the bike racer how he liked the new outer course around the city. He said he much preferred the inner course in the city.

Asian version of popular Tom Hanks movie: "Far East Gump."

At his wedding ceremony, the young man vowed to love, honor, and obey only one woman for the rest of his life. In case you're wondering, he married Minnie Moore.

American stops in the middle of a London street to observe the sights. Policeman yells, "Get your blooming arse out of the middle of the road." Flabbergasted, American looks around and says, "What horse?"

Madge asks Flo, "How's Bucky doing in school?" Flo says, "He's having trouble with his grammar." Madge responds, "Well, why doesn't she leave him alone and let the teacher handle it?"

Annette tells Audrey, "Poor Juanita's husband finally passed." Audrey says, "I didn't realize he was still in school."

Bank manager questions teller, "How's your new assistant doing?" Teller answers, "Okay, I guess. Right now she's going through the change." He responds, "Isn't she a little young for that?"

The new SUV with a mattress in the rear must be a Letsus.

Do you think Dr. Frankenstein borrowed a few of the body parts from Igor before he hired him?

Man and wife are at the beach with their thirteen-year-old daughter. Mom says, "Isn't Ashley cute in her little bikini?" Unhappy dad replies, "She looks like a duck. You can see everything but the quack."

He walked in to a bar and ordered a Cuba Libre. Bartender said he was out of Coca-Cola but could use something else. Customer replied, "If it ain't Coke, don't fix it."

Husband and wife are having a horrible time at breakfast. "Who peed in your cereal?" he asked. "I'm very suspicious," she replied, "and I'd advise you to keep an eye on yours."

The dog charged in to the kitchen wet and slobbering. Grandma nailed him with a cooking pan. When questioned, she said she was told to wok the dog anytime she felt like it.

After three communions in one day, the church altar was illuminated for the evening service. The minister was also well lit.

She went on a diet, and for three weeks, she didn't lose a pound. Then all of a sudden, good thins began to happen.

Connie tells Ethel, "You've just gotta change your dating habits. Mark deceived you. Frank dumped you. Ronny made fun of you. You really need willpower." "Oh," Ethel replies, "will you introduce me?"

Spring is the time when boys in school start thinking about what the girls have been thinking about all year.

When Catherine the Great seized power from Peter, she was just trying to empress everybody in Russia.

Little Jeremy was popping off at his mom during dinner. "Keep your mouth shut," she said, "and eat your spinach."

Two divorcees were having a drink. Myrtle said, "That Mort was lower than whale poop." Jordy countered, "Sounds like Eddie. He was a real bass turd."

Obnoxious airline passenger tells flight attendant, "Get me a blanket, get me some wine, get me my dinner, get me—" She interrupts, "I'll get you a parachute if you'll use it."

He loved his secretary and thought she was the best typist in the world, but he broke out in a cold sweat after she missed three straight periods.

Daughter says, "Mom, there's some kind of varmint on the floor in the kitchen." Mom replies, "Well, if you'll clean it up, I'll find out who's sick."

Someone asked several band members what it was like at the park concert when the big storm came up. Tuba player replied, "The answer, my friend, is blowing in the wind."

Ray asks Sid, "Do you believe in God?" "Do I believe in Him?" Sid answers. "I talk to Him every day. I even call Him by his first name."

Forty-year-old woman had a thirty-year-old boyfriend. A twenty-two-year-old girl swooped in and stole him away. Would you say the forty-year-old was outdated?

The couple was thrown out of the raw oyster bar on their very first visit. They thought they were supposed to eat oysters in the nude.

Immediately after blastoff, the module commander sent a frantic message back to mission control, "Did you remember to launch lunch?"

Dad says, "Our pastor is getting too old to drive. He had another fender bender today." Son inquires, "Is that why they call him the wreck-tor?"

The doctor wrote a book on medical procedures, but included some incorrect information in his references. As a result, he had to have his appendix removed.

Three giggly young girls are talking. The first one asks, "What is it they call a boy's thingamagig?" The second girl responds, "Are you talking about his whatchamacallit?" Third girl chimes in, "You mean his doolaly?"

Son is looking for his wayward dad and asks bartender if he's seen him. "Yeah," bartender says. "He left here about 10:30. Boy, has he got a way with the women." Son inquires, "How many?"

Husband complains to wife at bedtime, "I've got a stiff neck tonight." She replies, "Sometimes I think Mother Nature gets her priorities turned around."

Agnes asks Fran, "What is Freddie going to do for his summer vacation?" Fran responds, "He wants to go to see Antarctica." Agnes says, "And where does she live?"

Sixty-five-year-old man complains to his cronies, "Every time I have a chance to make love, I feel like I just got through making love."

In Robin Hood's time, it was not unusual for a lover's tryst to be settled by a cross beau.

Note: These words were meant to be pun-*ish* and not punish*ment.* Hope you had fun.

The End

CPSIA information can be obtained
at www.ICGtesting.com
Printed in the USA
FFOW03n1603010417
34018FF